CAT in the NIGHT

MADELEINE DUNPHY   ILLUSTRATED BY JOSHUA S. BRUNET

Web of Life

CHILDREN'S BOOKS

For information, write to:
Web of Life Children's Books
P.O. Box 2726, Berkeley, California 94702

Published in the United States in 2016 by Web of Life Children's Books.

Printed in Malaysia.

Library of Congress Control Number: 2015913953

ISBN 0-9883303-6-9 (hardcover edition)
978-0-9883303-6-8

The artwork for this book was prepared using acrylic paint, oil paint, and colored pencils.

For more information about our books, and the authors and artists who create them,
visit our website: www.weboflifebooks.com

Distributed by Publishers Group West
(800) 788-3123
www.pgw.com

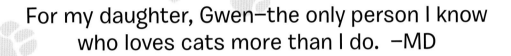

For my daughter, Gwen—the only person I know
who loves cats more than I do. —MD

To Cara, Caleb, Coleson, and Carter. And to Julia.
Thank you so much. —JSB

Special thanks to Coleson Brunet, age 7, for the child's drawing of a cat.

Rusty lies curled in a ball at the bottom of Gwen's bed.
He is waking up just as Gwen is falling asleep.

Quietly, Rusty slips outside through an open window. There he smells night-blooming jasmine, an overflowing garbage can, and the scents of familiar neighborhood animals. But tonight, something is ... different. It is the scent of an unknown cat. An intruder!

Rusty scans the yard. His excellent night vision allows him to see clearly, even in the darkest of shadows. Near the backyard fence he notices something move. He looks for the cat, but it is only a skunk scampering through the ivy.

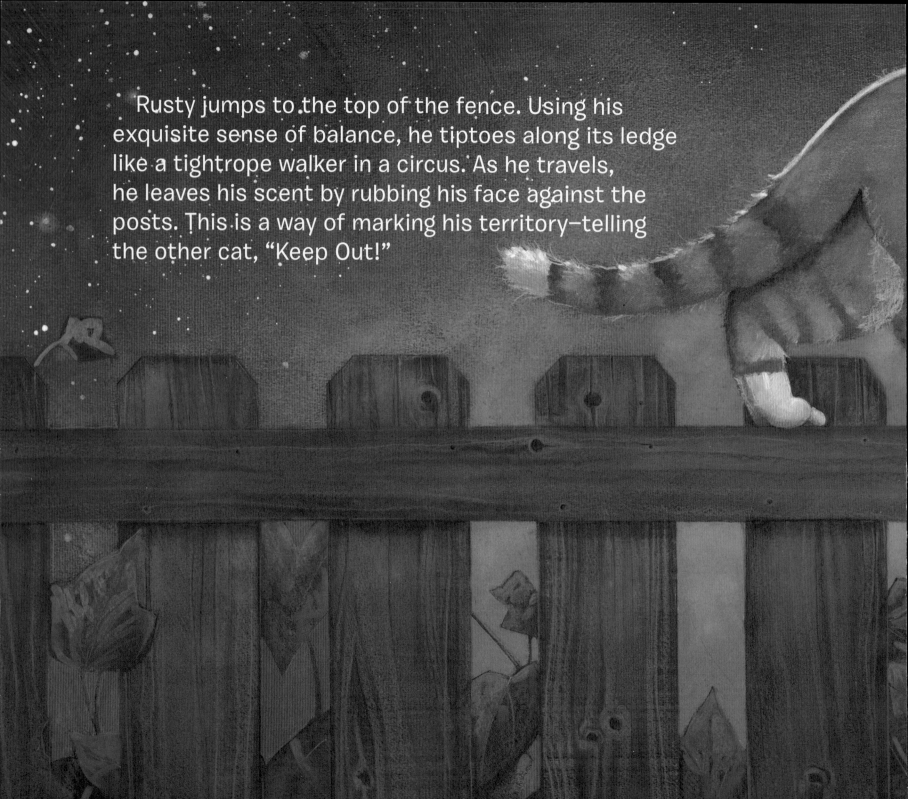

Rusty jumps to the top of the fence. Using his
exquisite sense of balance, he tiptoes along its ledge
like a tightrope walker in a circus. As he travels,
he leaves his scent by rubbing his face against the
posts. This is a way of marking his territory—telling
the other cat, "Keep Out!"

Sniffing the wind, Rusty picks up the intruder's scent and follows it to the next yard. But instead of finding the cat, he discovers two raccoons splashing in a child's play pool! He stops for a moment to watch them.

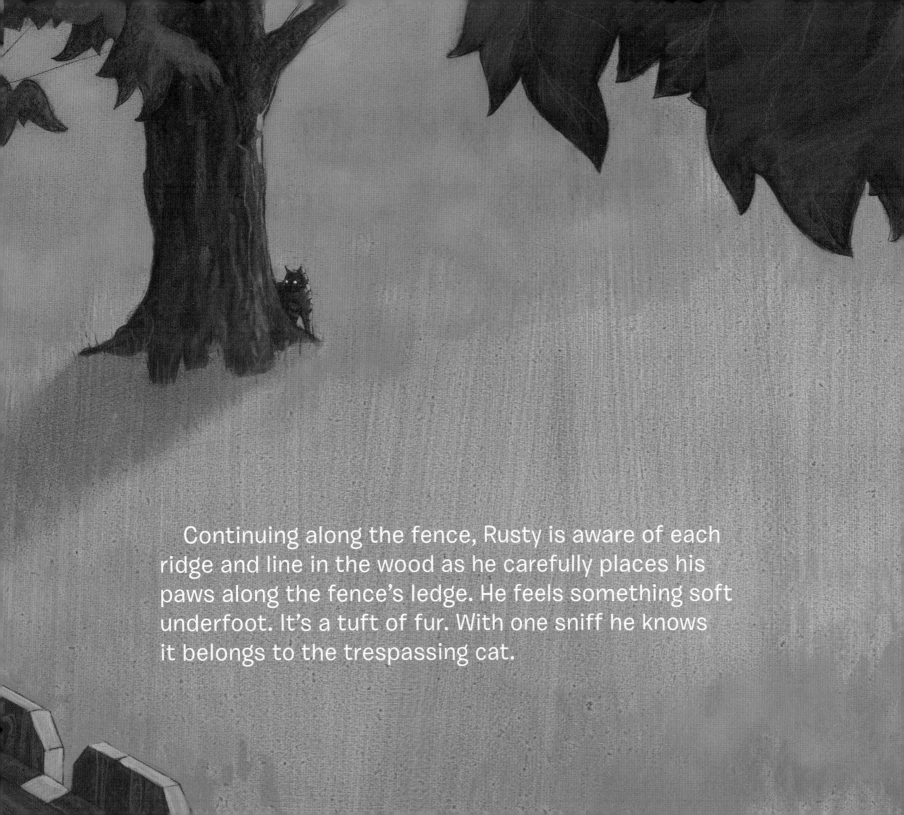

Continuing along the fence, Rusty is aware of each ridge and line in the wood as he carefully places his paws along the fence's ledge. He feels something soft underfoot. It's a tuft of fur. With one sniff he knows it belongs to the trespassing cat.

Rusty's ears perk up. He hears a high-pitched
squeak. Thump! He jumps down to the lawn.
His eyes focus on a tiny movement in the grass.
Slowly, one step at a time, he approaches.
His whiskers sweep forward, and ... pounce!

While cleaning his face after a mouse meal, Rusty glimpses something furry hiding behind a tree. At first glance, it looks like a cat. But it's an opossum. In the moonlight, her white face is ghostly. She is neither Rusty's predator nor prey, so he shows little interest as her ratlike tail disappears into the bushes.

Overhead, a scratching sound startles Rusty. He climbs to the roof of a garage to investigate. There he spies two eyes peering at him. It is the cat intruder!

Both cats arch their backs, fur standing on end. Rusty growls. The other cat yowls. They sing an eerie song.

Suddenly, their hissing and screeching is loud enough to wake the neighbors. Tufts of fur fly! Locked in battle, Rusty and his rival roll off the roof, flip around in midair, and then land on their feet.

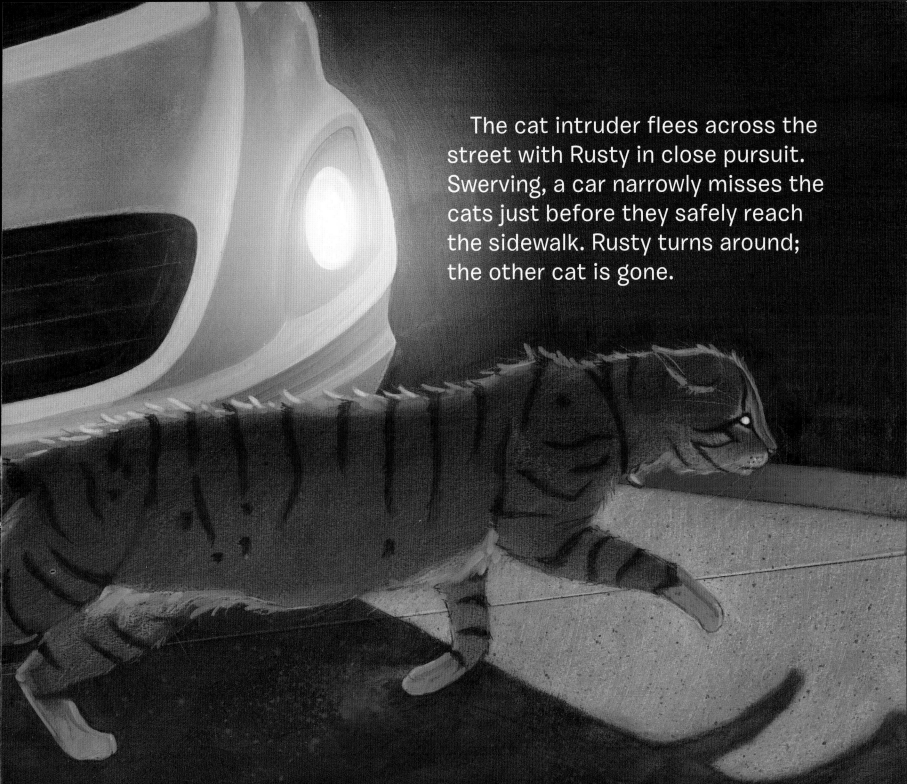

The cat intruder flees across the street with Rusty in close pursuit. Swerving, a car narrowly misses the cats just before they safely reach the sidewalk. Rusty turns around; the other cat is gone.

Rusty crosses the street again, but this time more slowly. There is a glimmer of light in the east, and he hears the stirrings of birds and other animals in the trees. A robin whistles his morning song—"Cheer-up! Cheerily! Cheer-up! Cheerily!"

Rusty jumps through the window, breathing in the familiar smells of home. First stop: food bowl. His name tag clinks against the bowl as he devours the remaining kibble.

Then, as if nothing happened, Rusty climbs onto Gwen's bed, calmly stretches, and settles into his usual place. Half awake, Gwen reaches down and strokes his soft fur. "Did you sleep well?" she asks. Rusty closes his eyes and purrs.

I LOVE RUSTY

MORE ABOUT CATS

Although cats have been living with humans for more than 4,000 years, their senses are still designed for living in the wild. After reading the information below, see if you can find the places in the story where Rusty uses his senses.

Hearing – Cats' sense of hearing is remarkable. Their hearing range extends two octaves higher than ours, about eleven octaves in total. This range allows cats to hear the ultrasonic pulses of bats and the high-pitched squeaks of mice and other rodents that we can't hear. They can even tell different types of rodents apart by their squeaks! Their mobile and erect ears also help cats to locate where sounds are coming from.

Vision – Cats can see in the near dark and can detect even the tiniest of movements. Cats can only see two colors, though: yellow and blue. Differences between objects, such as brightness, pattern, shape, or size, seem to be more important to cats than color. Cats' eyes can't focus any closer than about a foot (or 30 centimeters) away. To compensate for this, cats can swing their whiskers forward to create a tactile "picture" of objects that are close by.

Touch – Cats' paws are exceptionally sensitive; this explains why some cats don't like to have their paws touched. Both the pads on their paws and their claws are packed with nerve endings, which enable cats to feel exactly what is below their feet or in between their toes. The places where the whiskers attach to a cat's face are also very sensitive to touch. Cats frequently use their whiskers while hunting and to judge whether openings are big enough to squeeze through.

Balance – Cats have an extraordinary sense of balance. This is due to the vestibular system located in their inner ear. A cat's sense of balance is the most impressive when it jumps, slips, or falls. Less than a tenth of a second after a cat falls, it moves its head upward and rotates its neck so that the cat can look downward to land on its feet.

Smell – Like dogs, cats depend greatly on their sense of smell. Cats hunt by locating the scents of prey and by tracking smells that are blown downwind. Their sense of smell is so refined that they can probably distinguish between many thousands of different smells. Cats have an extra way to smell, called the VNO (vomeronasal organ). The VNO functions somewhere between the sense of smell and taste and is used mainly to detect the scents of other cats.

For more information about cats and their senses, please refer to the book **Cat Sense: How the New Feline Science Can Make You a Better Friend to Your Pet,** by John Bradshaw.